PANDED
ANION GUIDE

F LINARIA PART 1

L. MCNEIL

THREE DRAGON
PUBLISHING

First published in Great Britain in 2019

ISBN: 978-0-9957922-3-4

Three Dragon Publishing
www.llmcneil.com

Printed and bound in Great Britain by Clays Ltd, Elcograf S.p.A.

Cover artwork by: Omercan Cirit

Cover design by: Holly Jameson

Artwork by:
Trevor Smith Art
Art of Monztre
Katerina Moskvina
Omercan Cirit

Formatting by: Katie Pettit

WORLD OF LINARIA

NOVELS

Moroda

Palom

Amarah

NOVELLAS

Rise of a Sky Pirate

ACKNOWLEDGEMENTS

I would like to thank so many people for their unending support, patience, and help. But in particular, I would like to thank the freelancers, designers, illustrators, formatters, writers, and readers, without whom this guide could not have been created.

To Olivia and Pipkin, I cannot thank you enough for your encouragement.

To anyone who purchases this book, I am eternally grateful.

CONTENTS

The World of Linaria

Linaria is a world where dragons are revered as gods, where airships rule the skies, and where war is stirring.

From the rolling hills and meadows of Corhaven to the west, the alpine summits of the floating islands to the north, and the lush forests and deep valleys of Val Sharis to the east, the world is full of beauty.

With pirates and soldiers, smiths and princes, Linaria is a vibrant land with a deeply unsettled past and an equally ominous future.

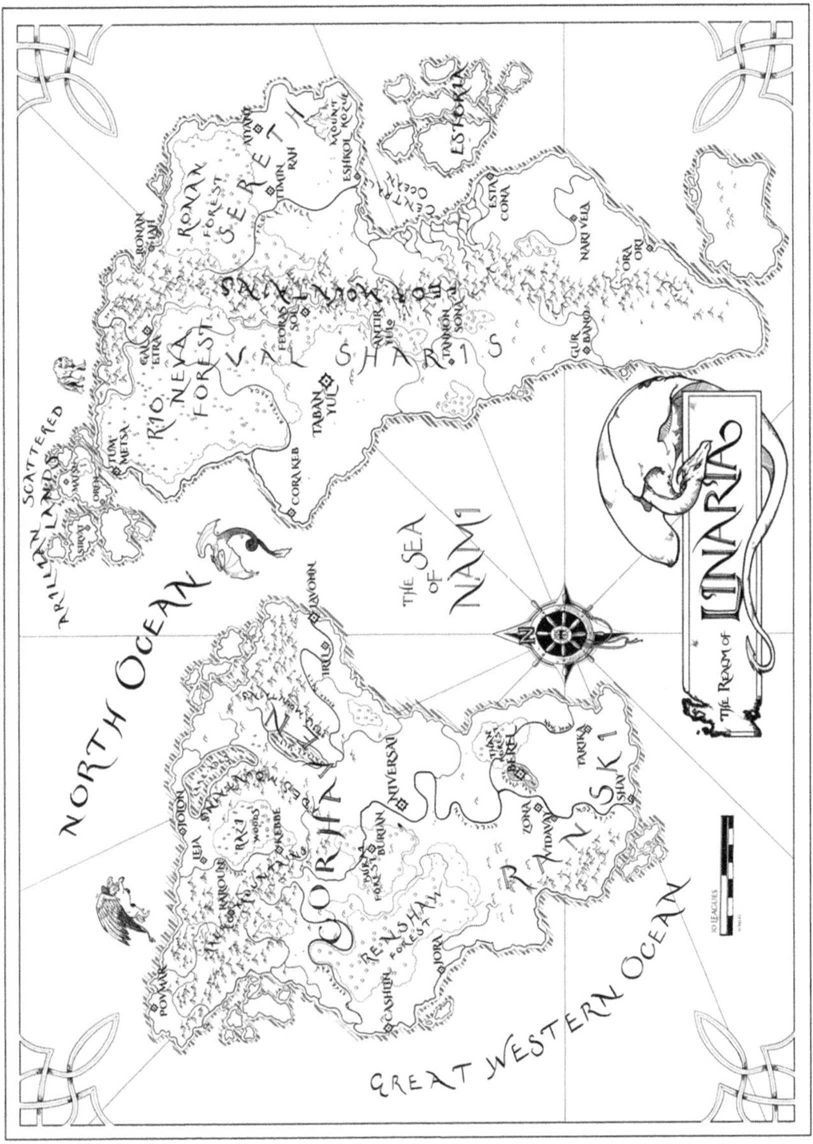
The Realm of Linaria
North Ocean
Great Western Ocean
The Sea of Nami
Scattered Arillian Lands
Central Ocean
Sereth
Valsharis
Gorhan
Ranski
Estoria
Rio Neva Forest
Ronan Forest
Realshai Forest
10 Leagues

Characters of Linaria

Linaria is home to eclectic characters from all walks of life across a number of different races, several of whom have a large part to play in deciding the future of the world.

PALOM

Discover the characters whose passage has influenced—and continues to influence—the dawning of a new age in Linaria.

ANAHRIK

Aciel

An Arillian vigilante, Aciel has taken it upon himself to seek retribution against Linaria for the crimes committed against his people in the Great War hundreds of years previous, where as a result, Arillians were banished from the mainlands of Linaria and pushed to the farthest reaches of the world.

Although weak by Arillian standards—the storms and lightning he creates are not particularly devastating—Aciel has the rare power of compulsion at his fingertips, and can manipulate others into following him, even against their wishes. With this unique talent, he has plunged Linaria into war and seeks to bring it to its knees.

His main tactic on his destructive campaign is to slay dragons and steal their innate magical power to boost his own strength. This behaviour is slowly tipping the balance of power within Linaria, but as long as Aciel can achieve his goals, it's a consequence he doesn't care for.

With his Generals Fogu and Jato at his command, he leads a growing army of both Arillians and people he has forced to submit to his will, simultaneously weakening his enemies and growing his own forces. He cares little for the consequences of his actions and the effect slaying dragons will have on Linaria, so long as his righteous actions restore Arillians to overlords.

Strategic, manipulative, and yet cowardly, Aciel uses his compulsion to force those who would oppose him to join his side and add people, weapons, and warships to his army.

ACIEL

Amarah

Amarah is the titular protagonist of book three in the World of Linaria epic fantasy series.

Thirty-six year old Amarah is an airship captain and sky pirate who cares for little other than herself. She doesn't believe in paying taxes or giving up her hard-earned gold to boost the wealth of those in power, and acts according to her own needs and desires.

Although born to a Samolen mother and half-Samolen father in the mage country of Ranski, Amarah was unable to tap into the innate magic of her people, nor could she read or write. Following her parents' disappointment in her, she was sent to the university in the Ranski capital, Berel, yet despite the somewhat vicious attempts by the scholars—known as Kalos—to teach her to read and the Samolen magic, Amarah remained unable to learn.

After years of shame and pain, Amarah fled Ranski and stowed away on airships to enter the neighbouring country of Corhaven in an attempt to live her life as she pleased, rather than per the wishes of her family. During her early teens, she drifted from town to town trying to gather enough money until she acquired her airship, *Khanna*.

Amarah wants nothing more than to fly the skies of Liniaria, free from anyone or anything holding her back, and she'll stop at nothing to get what she wants.

Bold, unsympathetic, and utterly fierce in everything she does, Amarah hates being in debt, and will do everything she can to ensure she remains free.

AMARAH

ANAHRIK

Anahrik is an Ittallan and Palom's business partner. He's a free-spirited silversmith who can transform into a falcon. He decorates Palom's weapons with fine silver and often charms potential customers into buying their wares with his fast talking.

Born into a trading family in the heart of Taban Yul, Anahrik is no stranger to the hustle and bustle of city life, fast-paced trading, or quickly building rapports with strangers to sell. He has a quick tongue and a speedy outlook, and it was no shock to his friends and family when his meraki enabled him to take the form of a falcon.

With a quick wit to match his physical speed, he often manages to persuade his customers to pay more than they normally would for his intricate silver works. Anahrik started in jewellery and decorative ornaments, but now works with Palom's weapons and armour, and the two have quite a signature shop.

Though free-spirited, he is quick to rise to a challenge, and Anahrik often relies on Palom to cool him down whenever negotiations go sour. The two are like brothers, and will follow each other to the end.

Confident, playful, and loyal to the end, Anahrik loves life and all that it offers. With Palom by his side, there is nothing he is afraid to do.

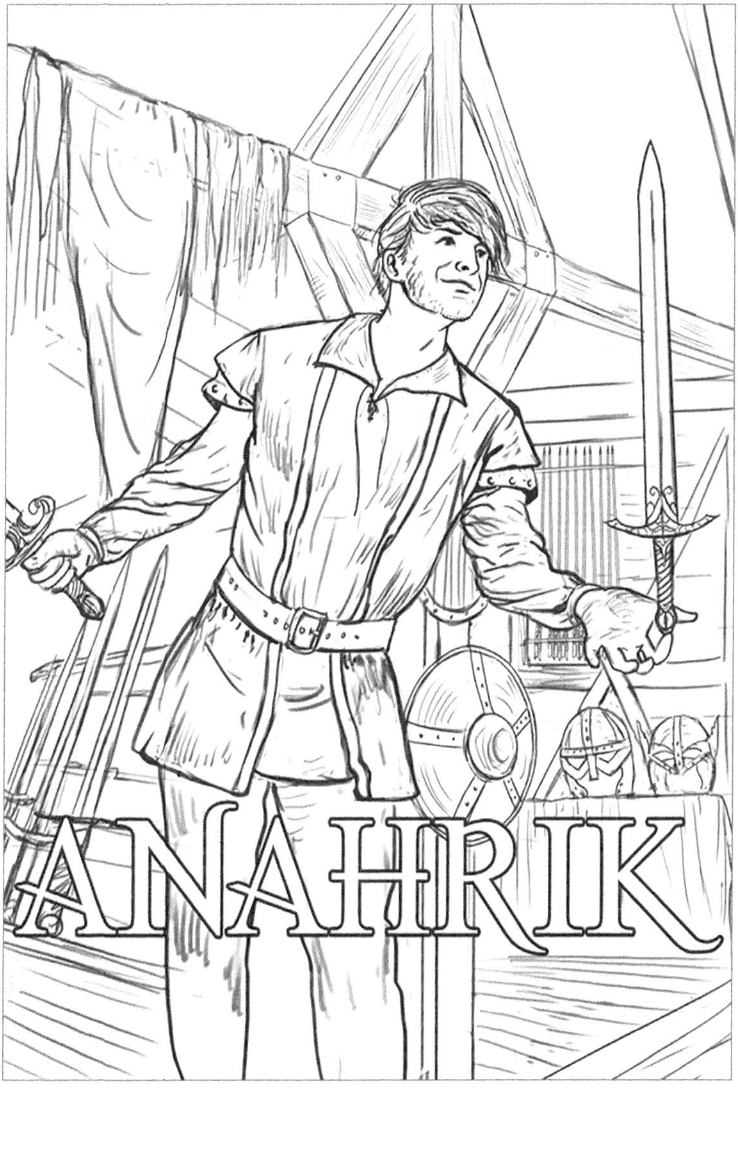
ANAHRIK

Antar

Sky pirate Antar was born in the tropical island nation of Estoria, far to the south-east of Linaria. He has a lean, muscular build and is an adept swimmer. Having grown up on boats of both the sky and sea, he's a competent pilot with a fearless, almost reckless nature.

Part of a small troupe of sky pirates who work for Traego, he pilots the airship *Otella*, though he aspires to have a ship of his own in the future. He works as Traego's second-in-command, with a fair amount of experience in aspects of strategising, flying, and fighting. He also has the rare attribute of being selfless rather than selfish, which leads many to trust his word perhaps against their better judgement.

He often scouts for Traego, looking for the troupe's next heist or treasure hunt. His fearlessness lends itself to the dangerous work, and he's been in more than his share of scrapes and tricky situations—if not against other pirates, then the Imperial Guard, or simply the wild creatures of Linaria.

Antar fights with a number of long daggers, of which he has four strapped across his chest and body. Although he isn't quick to anger, he's stubborn and will always see something through to the end.

Adventurous, confident, and clever, Antar won't back down from a challenge, and his physical prowess often sees him end up the better off when he's challenged.

ANTAR

ERYN

Eryn is a Goldstone, and Moroda's younger sister. She sees the world with a critical eye and will never rush headfirst into anything she hasn't first calculated. Her analytical mind often holds Moroda's dreams back, but as she is five years younger than her sister, she usually concedes to her elder's preferences.

Eryn, much like Moroda, has enjoyed a childhood full of luxury and more money than they knew what to do with. Now, through no fault of their own, their life situation has changed, and Eryn is trying to step up and keep herself and Moroda alive as they find themselves thrown in with people from all across Linaria. Although naive, she is less forgiving than Moroda, and has an arguably stronger survival instinct.

Despite occasional bickering, the two are closer than ever following the tragic death of their father, and Eryn has been responsible for keeping the pair from falling into complete ruin. She has the business mind of their father and wishes to continue his trade, though the two have met with little success thus far.

Though Eryn is more sensible, she is prone to the occasional emotional outburst when frustration or fear boils over. She cares about nothing so strongly as her sister and will remain by her side no matter the situation.

Practical, resourceful, and logical, Eryn keeps herself and her sister grounded, and is usually the voice of reason between them.

ERYN

Fogu

Fogu is a General in the Arillian army and answers to Aciel. Although under the compulsion of his leader, Fogu is an amazingly powerful Arillian, and far stronger than his leader. Formidable in battle, Fogu is well respected by both his comrades and enemies.

He's been in many battles, and the scars adorning his body are proof of his violent history. Fogu has the same abilities as most Arillians—he can conjure lightning and create storms—but in addition, he is able to attack with the wind itself; turning it as sharp as any blade and slicing at foes as if he wielded a thousand swords. It's an ability that makes him particularly deadly on the battlefield as he can use this attack from quite a range—as long as he has sight of his opponent.

With pale grey, almost blue wings, Fogu doesn't look physically threatening, but Aciel has harnessed the General's strength for his own gains and used Fogu primarily to wipe out those who won't succumb to his compulsion.

Although Fogu has spent recent years under the compulsion of Aciel, prior to this, Kohl saw him as more than just an ally, but a friend. The two Arillians are from the same remote village, Oren, and have both been "on-ground" to see how their people are treated by the rest of Linaria. It brings Fogu great shame to see how Arillians have acted and how people now think of them.

Old-fashioned, focussed, and somewhat placid, Fogu tries to do right by his superiors—even if he doesn't always agree with them.

FOGU

Isa

Isa is the titular protagonist of book four in the World of Linaria epic fantasy series.

Princess Isa is half-sister to both Sapora and Tacio—sharing the same father with her brothers, though they all have different mothers. As such, she is half-Ittallan, and half-Varkain, although she is more Ittallan than Varkain.

When she turned eighteen, she could tap into her inherent meraki and shapeshift—her true form is that of a wildcat, and indeed she spends much of her time climbing up buildings or leaping from tower to tower in the palace of Taban Yul, if not exploring the city by rooftop.

Because of her wildcat *meraki*, she is outright ignored by the Varkain, including her father, Vasil, who forbade her from travelling to Sereth with him, and yet shunned by the Ittallan of the palace, with whom she was forced to remain.

Never quite accepted into either place, Isa has found life difficult since tapping into her meraki, and has lost much of the respect owed to her by her birthright. Only Sapora—equally looked down upon by the Varkain for his mixed blood—had ever supported her and treated her as an equal. Her warrior father's battle savvy is not lost on her, and she can hold her own against more powerful opponents with ease.

Isa has been more of an outcast than a princess, and her explosive temper bubbles near the surface in retaliation. She longs to take steps to right the wrongs afforded to her and Sapora, and above all, to be accepted by her people.

Fiery, strong-willed, and independent, she dreams of the day she can wield the power she has desired since birth.

ISA

Jato

Fiancée to Aciel and one of the Generals in the Arillian army, Jato has been quite the formidable opponent to many characters in Linaria as she plays one of the key elements of the vigilante Arillian's campaign for world domination.

Other than Aciel and his conquest of Linaria, there is little she cares for, and in fact sees her fiancé's campaign as an extension of herself. Jato is in charge of the fleet of warships used to transport the ground troops who make up the bulk of Aciel's army, and takes the lead in the hunt for dragons Aciel kills. She takes her responsibilities seriously and rules with an iron fist.

As long as the job gets done, Jato doesn't care about the details. She treats most people as beneath her, and isn't above using force to get what she wants.

Quick to anger and quick to react, there aren't many who can stand against her power. She is especially dangerous when over water as she is able to create maelstroms which can easily overpower her foes.

Jato it utterly dedicated to her tasks and doesn't accept weakness in her comrades, happily cutting through them to get what she wants.

Vindictive, power-hungry, and scornful, getting on the wrong side of Jato might be the last thing someone ever does.

JATO

Kohl

Kohl is the titular protagonist of book five in the World of Linaria epic fantasy series.

Kohl is an Arillian—a race of winged people who can create lightning, have control over the wind, and can thusly cause devastating storms to both attack enemies and defend themselves.

Despite his severe, haggard appearance, Kohl is well-spoken, though he speaks rarely, and harbours immense power. He has dark, umber coloured wings and can also harness the power of ice through the Arillian frost-touch, resulting in devastating blizzards and vicious storms.

Currently in exile from his own people, Kohl doesn't associate with any Arillians, especially not Aciel and his retinue, although it doesn't stop others from mistrusting him. He works as a dragon hunter, and has deep knowledge of the beasts revered as gods throughout Linaria, though he says surprisingly little on them, himself, or how he came to know what he knows.

He has incredible strength and is formidable in battle, though he is a reluctant fighter and will only get involved during dire moments where there are no other alternatives.

Many believe him to be in league with the Arillian threat, and their rogue leader, Aciel, though he denies such conspiration.

Reserved, solitary, and knowledgeable, Kohl is more mysterious than most, giving almost nothing away about himself or his past, and yet seems completely dedicated to those he allies with.

KOHL

Lathri

Lathri is an Ittallan healer whose past is intertwined with Palom. Her true form is that of a short-eared owl, though she doesn't transform very often.

The daughter of an influential Ittallan who served on the Council, she suffered more than most when Sapora slaughtered those she cared about. As a result, Lathri wants nothing more than to protect her remaining friends and allies, whatever the cost. She sees Sapora, Tacio, and the Varkain as the biggest threat to not just Val Sharis, but the world, and takes it upon herself to prevent further tragedy.

Although Lathri has lived in the Val Sharis capital, Taban Yul, for her whole life, she spent six years in Berel where she studied at the university. Following her education in the Ranski capital, Lathri knows much of the Samolen magic as well as Ittallan and Varkain politics through her links with the Council.

A natural healer, her education boosted her abilities, enabling her to restore power and cure a great many wounds—even if things are life-threatening. However, her own power becomes drained if she isn't able to adequately rest after using her magic.

She wishes to see an Ittallan on the throne—Isa specifically—and abhors the Varkain race in general. Lathri is able to see the bigger picture and always has her people's best interests at heart, even if the means make her actions somewhat manipulative.

Influential, elegant, and dignified, Lathri is of the social elite, and she uses her reputation and prestige to motivate and lead other Ittallan in Taban Yul.

LATHRI

Mateli

An Ittallan of immeasurable strength, Mateli was Palom's first mentor, and greatest rival.

Able to transform into a crocodile through his *meraki*, he has spent so much time in his true form that many of his reptilian features spill over. Uninterested in Imperial law and powerful enough to stand against almost anyone, Mateli's only goal is to exact his revenge on Palom—who was responsible for his arrest.

And he'll trample over anyone to achieve it.

He has spent a number of years locked in the dungeons below the palace of Taban Yul for crimes most savage, and has in fact filled more than half of the city's mausoleums. A foul creature who does what he wants when he wants and doesn't care for the consequences, Mateli sees through every task to the end—an almost unstoppable force.

Formerly a Captain of the Imperial Guard, he first came to the Council's notice after reports began trickling through of using excessive force, particularly on new recruits. Although he kept crime levels down in Taban Yul through fear, when several members of the Imperial Guard perished during his overzealous rages, the Council tried to retire him after they considered him too dangerous.

Unrelenting, merciless, and ultra-aggressive, Mateli is a demon from not just Palom's past, but from Taban Yul's past.

MATELI

Morgen

Morgen is the titular protagonist of book six in the World of Linaria epic fantasy series.

Morgen is a young man of twenty-two who joined the Imperial Guard in the hopes of becoming rich and famous. Though he was promoted to officer within his first year due to his skill with a blade, life following orders isn't exactly what he'd thought it would be. He joins the others following the dragon's attack on the city of Niversai, and it doesn't take long before he realises he is quite out of his depth.

The youngest of six sons, Morgen left his hometown to seek his fortune at the Corhaven capital. Strong for his age, Morgen managed to hold his own under a group of squires serving under knights at the castle, and he was soon taken under the wing of their captain.

Coming from a poor family, Morgen had no quick route of moving up other than sheer hard work and determination. He dislikes the way the Imperial Guard is being run—and Corhaven, too, by extension—and does not always agree with his orders, much to his colleague's chagrin.

Although he will do as he is bid by his superiors, Morgen is upset to see more and more of the world fall into disarray and war, and resolves to do what he can to prevent more devastation.

Solemn, obedient, and kind, Morgen has been pushed around and forced to follow orders his whole life, and he's not sure how much longer he can keep it up.

MORGEN

Moroda

Moroda is the titular protagonist of book one in the World of Linaria epic fantasy series.

A twenty-five year old woman from the Corhaven capital city, Niversai, Moroda was a Goldstone until the passing of her father and loss of the family money.

She has lived a relatively sheltered life with her every need met, and is naive about much of her world and the people in it. She is incredibly trusting of others and avoids conflict wherever possible, and yet she also has a courageous inner strength and intelligence that helps her see the good in almost any situation or person.

Moroda is closer to her sister now more than ever following the death of their father, although she hasn't quite grasped the seriousness of their situation now the last of their money is drying up. Untrained in battle and inexperienced in survival, Moroda knows her life will become difficult, but she approaches the challenge with a naive innocence and enthusiasm.

She is filled with a deep wonder of her world now she has been thrust into it, but does not always understand or appreciate the dangers it presents. With a desire to do the right thing and learn about her companions and the dragons of her world, she wishes to understand her place in the hope of making Linaria a better place.

Compassionate, courageous, and a bit of a dreamer, Moroda is desperate to prevent war from sweeping across Linaria.

MORODA

Palom

Palom is the titular protagonist of book two in the World of Linaria epic fantasy series.

A blacksmith and Ittallan, Palom's "true form" is that of a tiger. Proud and stalwart, Palom is a beast of a man, towering at almost seven foot tall, and has an incredible strength which he uses to protect those he cares for.

Originally from the remote village of Feoras Sol in Val Sharis, Palom spent much of his youth mining as it was by far the easiest and quickest way of earning a living. He lost his older brother in an unfortunate mining accident, and decided to seek a new trade. Using the ore and metal he obtained, he headed towards the larger capital city of Taban Yul to seek out an apprenticeship in blacksmithing.

It was also when he arrived in Taban Yul and met Anahrik that he began to learn the common tongue to help with trade, which he still speaks with a heavy accent. He also met Lathri in Taban Yul, where they enjoyed a brief but passionate relationship. Blunt and to the point, Palom has an intense dislike for the Varkain and knows much of the Ittallan's history with them due to Feoras Sol's proximity with the Varkain country of Sereth.

Palom blames himself for not being strong enough to save his brother, and when he came of age, his guilt manifested itself in his *meraki* transformation that would give him the power he desperately sought: a tiger.

Hardworking, loyal, and stoic, Palom will do whatever it takes to protect those he cares for.

PALOM

SAPORA

Sapora is a Varkain, one of the most despised races in all of Linaria. Grey-skinned creatures with the ability to shapeshift into snakes, the Varkain are rarely seen above ground, and shunned when they are. The Varkain have a centuries-long rivalry with their brother race, the Ittallan and their history is littered with battles and conquering, the greatest war of which commenced five thousand years ago.

Calm and collected, Sapora's temper rarely flares. It is in fact his cool temperament that makes people so wary of him, and he boasts an arrogance befitting any of the social elite.

Sapora believes himself and the Varkain above all and often treats others with contempt. There is very little that he fears, and he delights in scaring those who annoy him. He travels alone, defending himself with his fangs and claws, and using his twin scimitars only in desperate situations.

Although he is cold towards most people who aren't Varkain, he holds a grudging respect for those who keep to their word or show promise in battle. He isn't so arrogant or stubborn to ignore particularly powerful individuals or creatures, but will always attempt to turn any situation to his own gain.

He hungers for blood and power in equal measure and often succeeds in getting what he wants through manipulation of those around him.

Single-minded, proud, and ruthless, Sapora's true goals are unclear, although he seems to only act for his own, personal benefit.

SAPORA

Solvi

A young Ittallan who has only recently tapped into her *meraki* and thusly discovered her true form, Solvi is from the village of Feoras Sol, deep in the Rio Neva forest. She's Palom's niece—the daughter of his deceased brother—and she has never met her uncle.

Having grown up on the border of Sereth, she's no stranger to the Varkain whom occasionally traverse the forest which encircles her village on their way to the Val Sharis capital, Tabal Yul. More at home in the trees than anywhere else, Solvi's agility and fearlessness often lead her to biting off more than she can chew.

Educated in the capital, and only a few years behind Princess Isa, Solvi looks up to Isa with reverence, and disdains those who would harm the princess or her family.

Solvi is an Ittallan, another type of shapeshifter. She can transform into a snow leopard. She's very young at only eighteen years old, extremely stubborn, and quite wild. She lives in a remote village in the forest and as such spends a lot of time up trees. She's usually barefoot and wears anklets, bracelets, and earrings of silver that jingle when she moves.

Athletic, daring, and intelligent, Solvi has taken the best from her cultural roots and her education to become a force to be reckoned with in the battle for Linaria's future.

SOLVI

TACIO

Tacio is a Varkain who can shapeshift into the royal *naja* form—a cobra. He's a prince and younger brother to Sapora, though he longs to rule.

The prince is extremely materialistic and vain, and is meticulous over his appearance—even going so far as to slick his hair back with oil. He will fight if he needs to, but doesn't like to get dirty and prefers to delegate the task to others.

He rarely leaves Sereth, and like most Varkain, prefers the dark tunnels of their underground country. Although he has visited his father's palace in Taban Yul once before and greatly enjoys the wealth, he cares little for the Ittallan who live and work there.

He grudgingly tolerates Sapora, and mostly ignores Isa, and the dynamic between the three siblings has been tenuous at best.

Tacio's rank means he is in charge of the Cerastes—guards—of Sereth, and runs it like his own, private army. Through them, he has many eyes and ears in many places, and there's little that happens in his territory without him learning of it.

Due to his royal bloodline and unlikelihood of ever ruling, Tacio is prone to bouts of boredom and moping behaviour, which rarely bodes well for any thralls nearby. He greatly enjoys the fighting sport many thralls are forced into, and has a bloodlust that rivals even his father, the warrior-king Vasil.

Aggressive, sadistic, and power-hungry, Tacio has taken a significant chunk of Vasil's battle lust.

TACIO

Topeko

Topeko lives in the mage city of Berel, and works as a Kalos—a scholar—to those attending the University in the hopes of learning magic

A Samolen, Topeko is at home in Berel—a small city in the desert country of Ranski—and wishes for nothing more than to teach and educate those who are willing.

He is a scholar of *Ra* magic, the life-blood of Linaria said to stem from the dragon Goddess Rhea herself. He has two crystals embedded in his cheek—the mark of any of Samolen descent or any who use magic—one of purple to showcase his standing as a Kalos, and one in blue to show his particular branch of *Ra* magic.

Topeko is a lover of peace, much like his home nation, and will do anything he can to help people, aid in their pursuit of knowledge, or simply provide them with warm hospitality. Always smiling, Topeko's eyes and jewels twinkle with energy, and he gives off a warm aura to those around him.

His history with Amarah is unknown to most, but he is perhaps the truest friend she has, and half-raised, half-educated her when she was sent to Berel by her parents.

He has a great deal of knowledge in the history of magic, and by extension the dragons, and passionately tells stories of both to any who will listen, be they Kalosai, tourists, or friends.

Kind, knowledgeable, and patient, Topeko epitomises the traits favoured by the peace nation of Ranski.

TOPEKO

Traego

Traego is a sky pirate, the leader of a troupe, and the captain of an airship, *Otella*. He was the first sky pirate whom Amarah met, and his was the first troupe she joined when starting out in a life of thievery.

Rare among other sky pirates, Traego's crew often stay with him a long while—far beyond a couple of successful heists. Despite having many associates and acquaintances who know him by reputation, he rarely shares much about his personal life. In fact, he's never told anyone where he was born or who his family are—if indeed he has any remaining.

A master negotiator, Traego can talk for Linaria, and has talked himself out of almost as many dangerous situations as he's talked himself into. He always has an eye for opportunity and looks at the bigger picture rather than short-term successes.

He plays by his own rules and subverts many of the expectations other sky pirates have of him, in part to keep his actions unpredictable. Traego often brings young, down-on-their-luck youths into his troupe to ensure there isn't any bad blood on his crew, and prevent rivalries with more experienced pirates.

Since acquiring *Otella*, Traego has never once been caught by the Imperial Guard and is incredibly proud of his clean record in the air.

Charismatic, shrewd, and calculating, Traego may have a sarcastic sense of humour, but shows real care for the well-being of his allies.

TRAEGO
NORTH OCEAN
SCATTERED LANDS
RONAN FOREST
SERETH
ESTORIA
OCEAN
LAVONN
NARI

Leillu

Leillu is a young dragon hatched while in the care of Ittallan Palom. Her scales are sea-blue and grey, and she has a bold, inquisitive nature.

About the size of a large house cat, *Leillu* was given a name that is a term of endearment in the Ittallan language, and literally translates to, "little one." Although the dragon continues to grow quickly, the nickname has stuck, and Palom will not refer to her by any other name—going so far as to introduce the dragon by that name to others.

Dragons are able to breathe fire within days of hatching, and *Leillu* is no exception. Her hatching came as something of a surprise to Palom, but the blacksmith has taken the dragon in his stride, and now *Leillu* is able to bring her flame to the Ittallan's forging to give his weapons a unique flair.

As dragons and people rarely mix, Leillu's behaviour is undocumented and developing from day-to-day. She seems to have grown fond of Palom, following him about like a young puppy and even going so far as to protecting him from those she feels are a threat, but whether she will remain with him, or bring devastation down upon him, is yet to be seen.

Intelligent, playful, and curious, Leillu brings joy to Palom, and provides him with the companionship he has sorely missed.

LEILLU

Magic of Linaria

Magic flows through Linaria from a number of sources, the most prominent of which is from the dragons which soar above the land and breathe fire as apex predators. The Samolen of Ranski are able to tap into this magic, which they call *Ra* and *He*, and use it to power their towns and cities.

SAPORA

ISA

The shapeshifting races—the Ittallan and the Varkain—can tap into their own branch of magic known as *meraki*.

Arillians have great, feathered wings and can harness the power of storms and lightning, and, in addition to their *meraki*, the Varkain have their own ancient branch of blood magic at their disposal.

Dragon-Samolen Magic: *Ra* and *He*

It is said that the Dragon Goddess Rhea created the world of Linaria, and the point of creation—within the mage country of Ranski—is the source of all magic.

According to the Samolen who populate this peaceful nation, "Rhea's breath" is the lifeblood of the world, and from where all magic grows. Any who live in Linaria can tap into this magic, under the right tutelage, but it is strongest by far in the dragons themselves. They believe magic is life, and have come to name it *Ra*, for the old word, "to create." This is why in some parts of Linaria it is traditional to add the prefix *Ra* to a name or place to denote new life or new beginnings.

He is the destructive side to dragons and powers their fire. Likewise, *He* is added as a suffix to names when there has been suffering, loss, or death. Its devastation goes against the Samolen culture, and practice of destruction magic is therefore forbidden.

Samolen magic instead is based around *Ra*, which is referred to as an ancient artform. Their strength in this magic comes from the acknowledged point of creation, concentrated into a lake of vast size which separates the capital city of Ranski, Berel, into two halves.

The Samolen teachings state that when the world was very young, the dragons created by Rhea were far more numerous than they are today. All dragons carry within their chest a stone, a pure, crystallised form of Rhea's breath—for all dragons are her children—which gives them their fire, strength, and longevity.

The older and more powerful the dragon, the larger the beast, and the larger the crystal they carry. But the Samolen have taken the notion of crystallised Rhea's breath from the dragons, and turned it to their own goals to defend and protect Linaria's history and knowledge.

Through harnessing Rhea's breath in the form of crystals, the Samolen are able to enhance their innate life magic and tap into the very source of magic every day. These crystals are embedded into their cheeks as jewels, which are split into six colours, each denoting a different speciality:

Purple - The teacher, or Kalos

White - The healer, Kalosin

Green - The musician, or Kaloset

Red - The conjurer, or Kalosuk

Yellow - The shaper, or Kalosol

Blue - The student, or Kalosai

A teacher has some understanding of each of the five specialities in order to instruct students in the basics of *Ra* magic. Shapers are able to manipulate the energy which already exists in living things and the world around them. Conjurers are able to create energy that was not there before. Musicians are a form of healer, able to fuel their magic into sound and heal without touch, whereas true healers may restore health and cure injuries.

Samolen teachings take place in the various universities throughout Ranski, with the largest and most prestigious university located in the capital, Berel. The power of Berel is legendary, chiefly through harnessing five enormous dragon stones found at the University courtyard in Berel Old Town—an obvious show of the Samolen power.

Meraki

Other than Samolen magic, which arguably stems from the dragons and Linaria itself, *meraki* is an ancient magic that comes from within.

Both the Ittallan and Varkain races are able to tap into this innate ability, which allows a user to transform into their "true" form. The Varkain will exclusively change into a type of snake. In the case of the Ittallan, it may be any other animal.

Meraki can be tapped into once a person comes of age, usually around eighteen years old. While *meraki* is heavily influenced by genetics and family history—such as birds or felines—the exact form is highly unique to the individual, and is based on the needs or desires of the person going through the transformation.

Someone who requires strength can take the form of a tiger—like Palom—although bears and bulls have a similar effect. Likewise, someone who is nimble or dexterous may change into a raccoon or ferret.

The Ittallan version of any creature is always far larger and more imposing than the wild counterpart. For example, Palom's tiger form is eighteen feet long, nose to tail, with strength far beyond any animal found in nature.

Although the Ittallan can take the form of an animal, they are unable to communicate with other animals, or other Ittallan in their true form, while they are themselves transformed.

Perhaps more intimidating is the Varkain transformation. Rarely seen outside their tunnel country, Sereth, few

Linarians have seen the true form of any Varkain, and fewer still have lived to tell the tale.

Much like their brother race, the Varkain's transformed states are far larger than the animal counterparts. Many of the more powerful Varkain can shift into snakes some fifty or sixty feet long, with the average at least twenty-five feet long.

There has been a long-standing debate as to which form of meraki is purer, or older. The Ittallan view the Varkain *meraki* as lost or sick, without the variance and flourishes that they themselves expect and enjoy. In return, the Varkain believe they are the true shape-shifters, with the Ittallan race the result of a mutation that split off from their reptilian forms.

The differences between Ittallan and Varkain are so great—from their appearance, languages, culture, and behaviour, as well as their *meraki*—that they are considered wholly separate races, rather one a subset of the other.

For the Ittallan, certainly, the form a person transforms into through their meraki is considered their true form, yet it has been known for many Ittallan to turn feral by spending too long in this altered state, and never return to society.

Equally, someone who spends either too much time, or not enough, transformed will often find their features twisted as if by the animal inside trying to push its way through.

Blood Magic

As one of the oldest races, the Varkain have a magic all to themselves, in addition to their version of *meraki*. Though often despised, this magic is ancient, powerful, and the Varkain have complete control of it: blood magic.

Blood magic is not accessible to all, in fact there are very few Varkain who are able to understand it, much less harness it themselves. These few blood mages are known as Valendrin.

The Varkain royal family and most highly ranking Cerastes are educated in the basics of blood magic, for it is their duty to understand and pass on their race's histories, but it is rare than any individual will dabble in more than the bare minimum considering there is always a Valendrin nearby.

At least one Valendrin serves the Varkain King at all times, though there is a small force of them dotted throughout Sereth. They largely live by their own rules, separate from the rest of Varkain society, while they study their art and increase their knowledge and power of it.

As such, the royal family, or any Varkain, often turn to a Valendrin to consult with them on matters of education, history, or power. The blood mages are incredibly long-lived, and it is not uncommon for a single Valendrin to serve three or four kings before they finally wear out their magic and succumb to an ashen death.

Through this longevity, the Valendrin have a better grasp than most on the history of the Varkain—and of Linaria itself—as there are fewer generations between events of the past and today.

Blood magic has long been despised throughout Linaria, and as the Varkain live completely separate lives to the rest of the world—chiefly because their home country of Sereth lies underground—it has enabled them to practice this old magic without any interference from those who would look down upon such an art.

Aside from being abhorrent—the most powerful spells require the life blood of an individual, resulting in vast numbers of deaths referred to as sacrifices—the power gained from accessing such an art is said to go against Linaria itself.

This is clearly seen with the greatly enhanced lifespan of a Valendrin, the physical appearance of one who studies and practices the magic for a considered amount of time, and the eventual loss of their innate *meraki*. A Valendrin not only loses their ability to transform, but are also unable to produce children, leaving them a shell of their former selves. Given these limitations, there are few Varkain who willingly choose to study this magic, and Valendrins are rather uncommon.

The study of blood magic reached its peak some five thousand years ago, during the height of the Varkain-Ittallan civil war, and the royal family turned to the country's Valendrin to aid in their country's defence. What is now known as the Old Guard were hand-selected Varkain, warriors chosen for their prowess in battle or strength of their blood magic.

The Valendrin were able to take four individuals from the Old Guard and turn them into the most powerful of all Varkain weapons: the Arks.

Arillian Frost-Touch

The Arillians are a race of winged people who can create lightning, have control over the wind, and can cause devastating storms to both attack enemies and defend themselves. They are responsible for much of the scarring across Val Sharis, caused through their massive storms which tore through the land. They are among the most deadly of all who live in Linaria, and several wars have not endeared them to many.

Banished from mainland Linaria following the Great War, approximately one thousand years ago, the Arillians fled to the most northerly reaches of Val Sharis, across the North Ocean to where the Everwinter rules. Here, their powers are the strongest and most formidable, for the first Arillians are said to have been born from the ice itself and so remain connected with it.

The power of their ancestors is referred to as the Frost-touch, and is passed down from leader to leader, through the generations. Only one Arillian may access the Frost-touch at any time, and on the death of that Arillian, it passes to the next—usually a child or relative.

Through both ice and storms, Arillians are able to see and communicate with one another over incredible distances. An Arillian can see through a storm to anywhere else in Linaria, provided there is also a storm there, too.

Typically, Arillians use no weapons save their own abilities, further distancing themselves from others in Linaria.

Of all the abilities of Arillians, their oldest and most powerful is their last defence—a vast army which stands guard over their scattered islands: the Ice Golems. Headless, four-legged, and four-armed, these creatures are massive chunks of living ice created from the Everwinter itself. They serve as both guardians and judges over Arillian culture, history, and behaviour.

The Ice Golems decide who may or may not be permitted to approach the Arillian home, and also issue commands—which all Arillians must obey. These great sentinels are responsible for protecting the Arillians, and are the reason why no army has ever been able to successfully invade or attack the Arillian islands.

Whichever Arillian currently has the Frost-Touch is considered the leader of their people, and is able to communicate with the Ice Golems to a certain extent. They are magic made living and do not speak or live as people do, but simply remain dormant, ready to judge or act when the Arillians or their Everwinter home is threatened.

They are observers more than anything, and do not involve themselves in squabbles or fights between Arillians. In fact, all history, the Ice Golems have only been involved a handful of times, and always at the current leader's behest.

Any Arillian may approach the Ice Golems, but only the leader may actually speak with them, and relay their thoughts and wishes.

Mystical Beasts of Linaria

The apex predator and, according to Samolen teachings, the source of all magic within the world, dragons are numerous, sacred, and utterly intrinsic to Linaria's life and future.

TACIO

MATELI

Worshipped as gods, dragons are one of the most powerful creatures in the world, able to bring life or death wherever they travel.

Dragons

How dragons are perceived largely depends on what part of Linaria an individual is from.

In Ranski, they are sacred, worshipped as gods, and considered the creators of the world. Their teachings form the basis of most educational systems across Linaria, and so many who study are schooled in this belief.

Corhaven and Val Sharis, allies with Ranski, largely believe the same as the Samolen do—that dragons are holy. Highly respected creatures, those in Corhaven and Val Sharis know them as powerful beasts to be admired from a distance, and avoided if possible. Many believe in the Dragon Goddess Rhea, their creation story, and even phrases such as, "dragons above," have found their way into common usage.

Dragons are more numerous in Val Sharis than any other country, mostly due to the steep mountains, deep valleys, and wild, varied landscape where they may hunt plenty of prey.

Due to their visibility, dragons are perhaps more respected in Val Sharis than in Corhaven, and many Ittallan revere them with awe and wonder. Interestingly, although dragons are considered animals, no Ittallan has ever been able to take the form of a dragon through their meraki. It is perhaps this difference that makes the Ittallan believe dragons are divine, and to slay one—even in self-defense—is to commit a great sin.

Dragons are a far rarer sight in Corhaven—especially cities and large towns. When one is seen, it is usually more of a threat than anything else, one which most of the Imperial Guard is unused to dealing with or defending against.

Sevastos

Older dragons are able to learn the common tongue and converse with people, should they wish to. This is quite rare, and those dragons who reach this age are often referred to with a title of respect: Archon. These dragon elders are peaceful creatures who care little for those who live in Linaria, preferring to live their own, solitary existence.

And yet those dragons still older than these are referred to as a Sevastos. While dragons continue to grow throughout their lives, a Sevastos is almost another creature entirely—their magic has transcended to such levels as they do not need to eat or drink, and can sustain themselves aloft for days at a time, without the need to rest.

Considered the living gods of Linaria, Sevastos dragons have long influenced the world's history. From their reverence to willing sacrifices and bestowing their immense power upon Linarians, the Sevastos' are considered by many Samolen to the living embodiment of Rhea herself.

Like any other dragon, the Sevastos' are uninterested in the affairs of Linaria, but have taken steps at several points in history to involve themselves to restore the balance of power to the world.

As one of the most powerful creatures in Linaria, many have attempted to harness their strength—the most successful of which has been the forging of the *Valta Forinja*. These are cursed weapons created with a Sevastos crystal, which provides formidable strength, though it feeds off negative emotions such as shame, guilt, grief, paranoia, rage etc.

Phoenixes

One creature that thrives off heat is the phoenix. These red and gold scaled birds are attracted to fire, and a constant flame is required to keep their eggs warm enough for their chicks to hatch. As such, wherever there are phoenixes, you can be sure there will be dragons nearby.

These birds are long-lived and considered immortal, for any death results in a new hatchling from the ashes. They are covered in vibrant scales which dull with age, although they have a plume of feathers on their heads and wings.

Phoenixes generally live alone, although older, larger dragons can produce more fire, which attracts more phoenixes, and it isn't uncommon to see a veritable flock following elder dragons.

They nest beside dragon lairs—or within, if they can manage it—to keep their own temperatures high and create the best location for their eggs and chicks.

Found with frequency in Ranski, and also in Val Sharis, these phoenixes tend to follow leser dragons and live with them at high altitudes. A hardy creature, their scales protect them from dragon-fire, although their feathers can catch alight. Those birds who fly too close to a dragon can be seen burning up, but most phoenixes will survive this.

Phoenixes will lay a small clutch of eggs, usually no more than five, which, like dragon eggs, must be kept in constant flame to hatch. The hotter the fires, the more quickly they will hatch, and it can take anywhere from a few days to three weeks of incubation before the chicks are able to free themselves.

Ereven spheres

The attraction of phoenixes to dragons is so strong that Samolen mages have been able to capture this and create an ornament to scry for dragons. Such an artefact hasn't been used since ancient times, and true ereven spheres are rare—fetching a high price. Many imitation ereven spheres adorn the houses of nobility, but do not contain a true phoenix feather and so cannot be used to scry for dragons.

Phoenixes are quite flighty, and need little encouragement to retreat whenever they feel threatened. This has meant the gathering of their feathers for ereven spheres has been a challenging task, for which successful missions are handsomely rewarded.

The feathers used in ereven spheres must come from the plume of a living bird, plucked and encased while it is still hot. Taking the feather from a recently deceased bird, or from a moult, will result in a substandard ereven sphere that may work for a time, but will soon become unusable.

The black market is rife with these imitation spheres, as it is nigh impossible to tell the difference just by looking at the feather. When fresh from the bird, the feather glows red-gold, but this colour fades over time, until it turns ashen grey.

Many less than scrupulous sellers often dye grey or black feathers to bright red in the hopes of fooling their buyers. As many who wish to buy such an artefact are doing so to grow their own prestige and display them in their homes, rather than use them, many buyers cannot tell the difference, nor do they care to—as long as it looks good.

History of Linaria

"From dragon-flame begun, from dragon-flame undone."

The Samolen speak these words in their histories, which states how Linaria came to be created, and how it will inevitably come to end.

Rhea, the Dragon Goddess, is the creator of Linaria. They believe her children, the "dragons above" spoken of, will be the ones to bring it to an end.

LATHRI

SOLVI

While it is not the only creation story, it is the one most widely believed—in fact, almost all Linarians speak of Rhea as their Goddess, if not all are aware the dragons are said to be the ultimate destroyers, too.

For Rhea is *Ra*: life, she and her children are also *He*: death.

ITTALLAN-VARKAIN WAR

The Ittallan and the Varkain are brother races, both able to tap into the magic of *meraki*, and both sharing the same continent, divided by the Feor Mountains. They hold a long-standing hatred of each other, stemming from thousands of years ago when they fought over land, resources, and gold.

Val Sharis is arguably the richest country in Linaria, with many mines providing gold, gemstones, and metal ore from which weapons and armour can be produced. Sereth is a far more barren land, as most of the surface had been wiped out when the volcano in the south-east of the country erupted.

The two races have always fought, and records differ on when they were officially at war with one another. As long as there have been Ittallan and Varkain, the two have been at each other's throats, and indeed several leagues of both Val Sharis and Sereth have belonged to the other at certain points in history, with who was currently dominating the civil war dictating who ceded ground to the other.

Both races have always attempted to dominate the other, and their fighting reached its peak five thousand years ago, when the Valendrins of Sereth produced four Arks. These were four members of the Varkain Old Guard who had undergone a blood magic ritual unlike anything in Linaria's history.

Twisted and shaped almost beyond recognition, the Arks were four immortal warriors capable of devastating the Ittallan and cementing the Varkain as the undisputed victors of the war.

The creation of the Arks changed the rules. Following their birth, the Ittallan experienced the worst devastation in recorded history. The Arks wiped out towns and villages with ease, slaughtering everyone they discovered and bringing desolation to Val Sharis.

Never before had the Valendrins' powers been used to such terrifying efficiency, and for almost a whole year, they led the slaughter. But not all Varkain agreed with the destruction, and many felt it was a step too far—what point would there be in winning the war if all they were left with was more barren land?

The only thing that could rival the Arks power was a Sevastos. While the history books are not clear on the details, shortly after a Sevastos was seen in the skies above Val Sharis, the Arks vanished.

After the Arks disappeared, the Ittallan and Varkain settled into an uneasy peace as both nations attempted to rebuild from the generations-long war. Val Sharis recovered far faster than Sereth given the abundant gold, and their trade routes with the western continent aided in their growth.

The war officially ended some forty years ago, when the Varkain warrior-king, Vasil, attacked the Ittallan capital with a handful of his best Cerastes. They slaughtered the Ittallan royalty and conquered Val Sharis in a single, bloody night. Vasil elected to remain in Sereth while he put in place a ruling council that would govern the Ittallan in his stead.

Val Sharis therefore pays homage to Sereth annually, but have been spared further bloodshed and destruction following Vasil's conquest. His children by two Ittallan women—Sapora and Isa—are the first generation to formally bring the two races together.

THE GREAT WAR

Linaria's history is fraught with bloodshed, and the Great War brought with it destruction to the entire world. It began when the devastation wrought by the Arillians became too much, and too many people were injured or killed in their violent storms.

Although the Arillians were more interested in their own conflicts than turning their powers on the rest of Linaria, there were still many thousands of people caught up in their tantrums and the resulting damage to farms, cities, and land, forced the world to step up and do something about the constant fear of thunderstorms.

When Arillians lashed out at one another, the storms, hurricanes, and tornadoes they produced were nigh unstoppable. Many cities attempted to reason with the Arillians by sending out envoys or offering gifts. Others threatened them with violence, or cut off their trade routes to squeeze out a preferred behaviour.

A law unto themselves, however, the Arillians found it easy to simply fly away and do business with other places across a more forgiving part of Linaria. Chiefly they remained within Val Sharis, but many crossed the Sea of Nami to Corhaven—though they had no way to access the Samolen of Ranski given their rules against violence and bloodshed.

But for close to a decade, relationships between Arillians and the rest of Linaria grew ever more tense.

Something had to give.

The Imperial Guard

When the difficulties grew too much to bear, the ruling council of Val Sharis and the King of Corhaven joined their forces together—made up of royal guards, palace fighters, and the knights who looked after the common folk. Mercenaries from across both nations joined the growing army, and the force swelled to become the Imperial Guard.

Uniformed in red and gold livery, whether from Val Sharis or Corhaven, the Imperial Guard shared a common purpose—to protect their countries and citizens from any who might harm them, and uphold the laws. During the Great War, this was chiefly against the Arillians, and it was the Imperial Guard who were ultimately responsible for driving them back.

Though there are differences between the Imperial Guard depending on which country they are from—for example the Ittallan favour protruding spikes on the helmets of their captains, whereas feathered plumes are more likely to be found on Corhaven captains.

In addition to protecting Linarians from aggressors, the Imperial Guard also enforces the laws of the land, with factions and outposts in almost every town and city throughout Corhaven and Val Sharis. Charged with seizing criminals, enforcing taxes, and carrying out the duty of the council or king, there is much to do in the Imperial Guard, no matter your rank.

And in times of strife, they manage the efforts to rebuild damage, and are often the first place citizens turn to when they need help.

The Arks

Immortal warriors created by the blood magic of a Valendrin, the four Arks are named; Karekis, Veynothi, Malashash, and Brahm.

Brahm had been a Valendrin himself before his transformation, using his abilities to develop a way to control the creatures of the land and sea to do his bidding. While not a particularly powerful warrior, the Varkain royalty wanted a Valendrin in the Old Guard, and indeed when the creation of the Arks became a possibility, Brahm was thrust forward. His experiments with creatures were not all unsuccessful, and today, many Ittallan on the coast cower at the mention of Brahm's monster.

Malashash had been a protector of Sereth, and defended the country from counterattacks while his comrades and the Old Guard waged war against the Ittallan. Malashash lived a life alone from most Varkain at the base of the Feor Mountains, and through the Valendrin's magic, was able to absorb much of the iron ore found at the site, which boosted his defensive abilities until he was almost invulnerable.

An aggressor within the Old Guard, Veynothi fought on the front line and has been responsible for the deaths of more Ittallan than any other. The Valendrin were able to harness her merciless attacks and give her the power to absorb the strength and life energy from those near her. She grows stronger with every life she takes, and her name strikes fear in the hearts of many who hear it.

The final Ark, Karakis, had been a Varkain prince. With no powers of his own, he'd never meddled in blood magic until a Valendrin transformed him. He was the first Ark, and was given strength twice that of those who followed him. Originally an unwilling fighter, but one who was ruthlessly efficient once an Ark, Karakis was forced into the transformation by his mother, the Queen, who wanted her son to prove his worth as the Ittallan-Varkain war heightened.

The Arks reigned supreme on the battlefield, and pushed all Ittallan from Sereth to reclaim their lands. For nearly three years, the Arks turned the tide of battle in the war, lifting the Varkain from the edge of defeat and handing victory into their claws.

The Varkain, and the rest of Linaria as they looked on, believed the war was won. There was nothing that could stand up to their warriors. Even if they were overpowered, they were immortal, and could not be killed by any weapon or fang.

And so when they vanished from the face of Linaria without warning, the war ground to a sudden halt. The Ittallan were too weak to press forward, and the Varkain had relied on their secret weapons for so long, they held back. The remaining Valendrin explained they had been punished by the gods for their magic, and refused to create new Arks for fear their whole race would be struck down in the same way.

The creation of the Arks changed the rules of warfare, and their sudden disappearance has long been considered a stroke of luck.

Themes of the Series

The World of Linaria is an epic fantasy series that boasts an eclectic cast of characters, exciting types of magic, and plenty of dragons.

But beyond the light-hearted fun, the series touches on many themes:

Staying true to oneself. Overcoming adversity. Sacrifice. Inner demons—both facing them and succumbing to them. Isolation. Fear and hatred. Bigotry and prejudice. Friendship. Determination. Brotherhood and sisterhood.

These all become ever more apparent, especially in part two of the series with books four, five, and six.

The stories show that you can be as powerful as a tiger and still hit rock bottom. You can be born with all the money you'll ever want or need and still end up in prison. You can be as humble as a farm boy and youngest child, and still rise to greatness. You can be royal and powerless. You can be surrounded by friends and still feel alone. You can forge your own path and be seen as a leader or a vigilante.

And ultimately, the series shows that the world—and people—is not always what it seems.

Author Note

Thank you so much for reading this *Expanded Companion Guide*, I hope you enjoyed it!

If you can't wait to get back to the *World of Linaria*, sign up to my mailing list and you'll be the first to hear news, announcements, and special offers.

You'll also receive a high-res digital map of Linaria and a free spin-off novella—Rise of a Sky Pirate—just for subscribing! You can also buy books and bookswag on my website directly if you'd like to support me.

www.llmcneil.com

My novels are available as audiobooks on Audible. Grab your copies now and hear the *World of Linaria* brought to life by Georgie Leonard!

GLOSSARY

Airship: Vessel used as a means of transport for both passengers and cargo. Developed from sea vessels of old, boasting the power of flight. Available in various designs, shapes, and sizes depending on their purpose.

Arillian: Race; winged people from the far north. They have the power over wind and lightning, and can create vast storms. Some have additional powers, such as ice.

Berel: City; capital of Ranski, the Samolen homeland. Home of the university where magic is taught by scholars.

Burian: Town; small town to the west of Niversai, surrounded by forest.

Cerastes: An elite fighting caste of Varkain who report to their King and defend Sereth from intruders. They can transform into vipers.

Corhaven: Country; located on the western continent.

Crown: Currency; large, six-sided gold coin with a warship emblazoned on each side. Available as triple, double, single, and half.

Dragon: Animal; wild beasts which roam Linaria, supposedly descended from the Goddess Rhea herself. They are revered as gods and feared by many.

Ereven Sphere: Ornament; a small, glass sphere with a phoenix feather inside, originally created by the Samolen to locate dragons.

Florin: Currency; medium-sized, eight-sided silver coin with a set of scales emblazoned on each side. Available as triple, double, single, and half.

Human: Race; people from the western continents.

Imperial Fleet: The collection of warships and scouting airships under the control of Corhaven and Val Sharis, numbering some five hundred. Each warship allegedly cost 30 Double-Crowns.

Imperial Guard: The soldiers who make up the fighting force and guard of the Imperial Alliance—the countries of Corhaven and Val Sharis.

Ittallan: Race; people from the eastern continents. They have the power of meraki and can transform into animals.

Linaria: The name of the world.

Naja: An elite cast of Varkain who are typically always royals. They transform into cobras. Niversai: City; capital of Corhaven.

Penny: Currency; medium-sized round coin of dark iron, with a mill emblazoned on each side. Available as a penny and halfpenny.

Phoenix: Animal; scaled bird with vivid orange-red plumage. They follow dragons and are attracted to their heat. Their feathers can be used to find dragons.

Ranski: Country; located on the western continent, the Samolen homeland.

Rhea: A four-eyed dragon, the Goddess and creator of Linaria according to lore.

Rosecastle: The name of the castle in Niversai, home to the royal family.

Samolen: Race; people from the western continent. They have the power of magic hailing from the dragons.

Sea of Nami: A large body of water dividing the eastern and western continents, covered in trade routes by air and sea.

Sereth: Country; located on the eastern continent, the Varkain homeland.

Sevastos: An ancient dragon, the oldest and most powerful of all types.

Shingle: Currency; small, plain round coin made of iron.

Taban Yul: City; the largest city in Linaria, capital of Val Sharis, and the birthplace of trade. All of Linaria's currency is minted here.

Timin Rah: City; capital of Sereth.

Val Sharis: Country; the largest country in Linaria, located on the eastern continent, homeland of the Ittallan.

Valendrin: A Varkain blood mage who has mastered this ritualistic magic.

***Varkain*:** Race; people from the eastern continent. They have a power similar to meraki and can transform into snakes.

Warship: Large class of airship, designed specifically for defence. Fitted with heavy artillery and often crewed by members of the Imperial Guard.

About the Author

Lauren lives in a small village in Oxfordshire, studied Psychology at Brunel University, and has a fascination with MBTI (she's an INFJ).

Her debut epic fantasy series is *The World of Linaria*, a six-book series with an eclectic cast of characters and full to bursting with dragons, sky pirates, and airships!

She writes professionally as a Copywriter and has worked in Marketing for a number of years. Writing for a living has been a dream of hers since childhood, and being able to now do this gives her absolute joy.